Susan Gates

Pet Swapping Day

Illustrated by Lucy Keijser

Hippo

For Robert

JS/A 79799

Scholastic Children's Books,
Commonwealth House, 1-19 New Oxford Street,
London WC1A 1NU, UK
a division of Scholastic Ltd
London ~ New York ~ Toronto ~ Sydney ~ Auckland

Published in the UK by Scholastic Ltd, 1996

Text copyright © Susan Gates, 1996
Illustrations copyright © Lucy Keijser, 1996

ISBN 0 590 13988 6

Typeset by Backup Creative Services, Dorset
Printed by Cox & Wyman Ltd, Reading, Berks

10 9 8 7 6 5 4 3 2 1

S A 49799.

J   S/A 49799

LEABHARLANN CHONTAE MHUIGHEO

Five more *brilliant* Young Hippo School stories:

Or dare you try a Young Hippo Spooky?

Chapter 1

Corinne checked her list. It said:

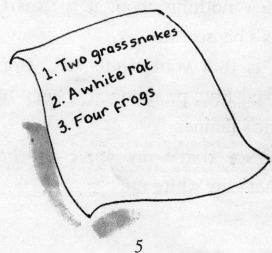

1. Two grass snakes
2. A white rat
3. Four frogs

It was pet swapping day at Parkside School. It happened once a term. Corinne, who was a very efficient person, organized it. And the teachers knew nothing about it. It was Class Six's big secret.

"Is that your white rat?" Corinne asked Eric, prodding at a lump under Eric's jumper.

"No, that's my apple for break. *That's* my white rat."

Eric's rat poked his head out of
Eric's trouser pocket. He grinned at
Corinne with his sharp little teeth
then disappeared again. He looked like
a very intelligent rat.

"And what do you want to swap him
for?" asked Corinne.

"I don't know yet," said Eric. "I've got my eye on those snakes that Adam's got in his lunch-box."

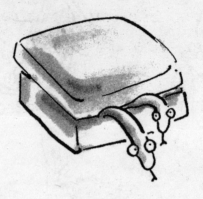

Corinne let Eric help her on pet swapping day. This was very kind of her. Because, although Eric loved helping, he wasn't very good at it. He wasn't a tidy-minded person like Corinne. He was a muddle-minded person. He attracted muddles like a dog attracts fleas. He just couldn't help it.

A little shrimp of a boy crept up to them. He was nervous about talking to Corinne. Corinne was the boss of Class Six. She sorted out everyone's problems. She was probably the most important person at Parkside School. And that's including the Headmaster.

"What do you want to swap?" asked Corinne kindly.

The shrimp held out a matchbox.

"What is it?" asked Eric. "Is it something interesting? I might swap my rat for it, if it is!"

The small boy slid open the matchbox. He let Eric peek inside.

"It's a beetle!" said Eric, disappointed.

"It's not just any old beetle," corrected the boy. "It's a dung-beetle!"

"And what's that in the matchbox with it?" asked Eric.

"I don't think I want to know that," said Corinne.

"It's a bit of cow-pat," said the small boy, keenly. "That's what they mostly feed on. Cow-pats."

"How disgusting!" cried Eric, looking rather green. "I'm not swapping my lovely white rat for something that eats cow-pats!"

"Well, I think my dung-beetle is lovely," said the small boy, in a hurt voice. "And he's ever so interesting. You could watch him all day. You ought to see the way he rolls the dung up into a little ball and then he—"

"I'm sure we'll find something to swap him with," interrupted Corinne quickly. And she wrote down

One dung-beetle on her list.

"What have you brought?" asked Eric, as a pale, skinny boy approached.

He was holding out a paper bag at arm's length. The top of the bag was screwed tight. And the bag rustled and jumped in a very sinister manner.

"Have you got any boa constrictors?" asked the pale, skinny boy. His eyes were shining with enthusiasm. "If you have, I'll swap these for it."

Eric was curious. He reached out for the bag.

"Careful!" warned the skinny boy. "They're dangerous. They might get nasty!"

"What are they?" asked Eric.

But the skinny boy didn't answer. "Got any piranha fish then?" he asked.

Corinne checked her list.

"No," she said. "Not today. We got a dung-beetle though."

The boy with the paper bag looked disappointed. "That's not very dangerous," he said, and wandered away.

A bell rang *BRINGGG!*

"I should've found out what he had in there," said Eric. "But it's too late now. School's starting."

"Hello, Miss!" Eric called out his usual cheery greeting as he bounced into the classroom. Then his hand flew to his mouth. "Whoops!" he said.

For Miss Walker wasn't there. In her place was a new, young teacher. He had yellow, floppy hair and pink cheeks. He had a new briefcase, shiny as a conker. And red pens bristled in his pockets.

He looked nervous. He had been warned that Class Six could give teachers a hard time. He had particularly been warned about a boy called Eric.

"Sit down, Class Six!" ordered their new teacher in a stern voice. He looked at them with hawk-like eyes.

He was ready for trouble. "As you can see, I am not a Miss. I am a Sir. My name is Mr Perry. And I shall be teaching you for the next few days."

Chapter 2

On other days, Class Six would have shouted out lots of questions. Like, "What did you say your name was?" and "Where's Miss Walker gone?" They would have started a loud conversation amongst themselves.

But today was pet swapping day. And on pet swapping day Class Six behaved like little angels.

Mr Perry said, "Get out your English files."

"Yes, Sir. Right away, Sir!" chorused Class Six obediently.

Eric's jumper seemed to have a life of its own. It wobbled with squirming lumps. First a lump popped up here, then there. There were strange bulges all over his body.

Corinne frowned at him.

"It's not my fault!" Eric mouthed back at her. "It's my rat! He's a bit lively today. I can't help it."

That was Eric's motto: "I can't help it." He was always saying it. When he found himself in a muddle he would cry: "I can't help it!" And usually, he couldn't.

Mr Perry opened his shiny new briefcase. He chose a red pen from his pocket. He looked at Class Six. All he could see was the tops of their heads. They were busy working.

Mr Perry began marking some books.

Squeak, squeak!

Mr Perry's head shot up. "Who's making that noise?"

"What noise, Sir?" asked Class Six, their eyes wide and innocent.

"That *squeak, squeak*. Didn't you hear it?"

"No, no, Sir, we didn't hear it," chorused Class Six, shaking their heads very hard.

Mr Perry carried on marking.

From Eric's cuff an intelligent, whiskery face peered out.

Mr Perry raised his head.

The face vanished.

Mr Perry looked down again.

Two seconds later two clever, pink eyes poked out the neck of Eric's jumper.

Mr Perry looked up.

A tail whisked away down Eric's sleeve, so quickly that your eyes couldn't follow.

Plop. Something green with goggly eyes hopped from table top to table top. *Plop.*

This happened every time. On every pet swapping day things escaped. Class Six's classroom was full of little scuttling things. Of chirps and squeaks and pitter-pattering feet. Miss Walker was a dreamy person. She floated round the classroom. She never noticed the muddle all around. She was Eric's favourite teacher.

But Mr Perry was different. He was on red alert. His eyes narrowed suspiciously. "I'm sure there's something going on here," he snapped.

A paper bag on a desk rustled.

"What's that?" cried Mr Perry, his eyes swivelling wildly.

"Nothing, Sir. Nothing," said Corinne, in her most soothing voice.

"It's only my lunch, Sir," said a pale, skinny boy. And he screwed up the neck of the paper bag extra tight. "It's all right, Sir. It can't get out."

Mr Perry shook his head in a bewildered way. He looked down again at his books.

"Whoops!" said Eric. He had been taking a peek in Adam's lunch-box. Checking to see if those snakes were a good swap. But he opened the lid a little too far. Before he could stop it a flat, scaly head slid out. A pair of unblinking eyes stared at him. A tongue flickered.

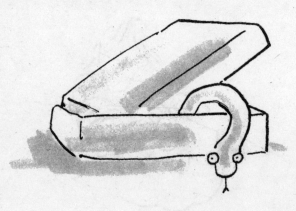

The rest of the snake flowed out. It flowed smoothly across the desk. Eric tried to grab it. But, naturally, he missed.

Class Six watched, fascinated. They held their breaths. They were so quiet you could hear a paper-clip drop.

The snake slithered over the desks towards Mr Perry. He marked away. Tick, tick, cross, cross went his busy red pen.

"Oh, no!" Eric's hand flew to his mouth in horror. The snake poured off the desk in a silvery trickle. Right into Mr Perry's open briefcase.

"It's not my fault," whispered Eric. "I couldn't help it."

BRINGGG! went the bell for break.

Mr Perry stood up. He snapped his shiny briefcase shut. He strode out of the room.

I can't understand what all the fuss is about, he was thinking. Why, apart from some rather strange noises, Class Six are no trouble at all!

"You've stolen my snake!" cried Adam. "Give me my snake back!"

But Mr Perry didn't hear him.

"Never mind," said Eric, cheerily. "You've still got one left."

Corinne updated her list.

One
~~Two~~ grass snakes

"Oh, by the way," said Corinne. "I'm going to the dentist's after break. My mum's coming for me. Don't worry – I'll be back at lunchtime to arrange the swaps and everything. But until then, you, Eric, are in charge of pet swapping day."

"Me?"

Eric could hardly believe his ears. A brilliant grin lit up his face like sunshine. "Me?" he said again. "I'm in charge?"

"Yes," said Corinne. "And just don't make a muddle of it, right? Here's the list. And make sure no teachers find out what's going on. Because if they do, pet swapping day will be cancelled – for ever."

"Don't worry! You can trust me!" cried Eric, eagerly hopping up and down. He couldn't wait to start being in charge. "I'll make sure nothing goes wrong!"

And he waved to Corinne as her mum took her out the school gates.

Chapter 3

Eric was thrilled. This was his big chance. He wanted to tell the world! Two clever pink eyes peered out of his cuff. "I'm in charge," Eric told his pet rat.

The tiny boy with the matchbox crept up to Eric.

"Where's Corinne?" he asked.

"I'm in charge," said Eric. It felt good saying that so he said it again. "*I'm* in charge of pet swapping day," he said, tapping his chest.

The small boy looked doubtful. "Well, if you're sure…" he said. "Only, I got two dung-beetles to swap now. I found another one."

"Have you? Where did you find the other one? No, don't tell me," said Eric.

Neatly, he changed his list.

Two
~~One~~ dung-beetle

He felt very business like and efficient. Corinne would be proud of him.

He folded the list up and stuck it behind his ear, so he wouldn't lose it.

There was a piece of spearmint gum behind his ear already. How long had that been there? He'd forgotten all about it. He popped it into his mouth and chewed happily.

Mr Perry strode across the school yard. He stopped, and opened his briefcase. He seemed to be looking for something.

"*Aaargh!*"

He leapt backwards, flinging his briefcase away.

"A snake! A snake!"

Eric rushed up. "It's okay, Sir, really! It's not an adder, Sir. It won't hurt you. Snakes like warm, dark places, Sir," said Eric, in an informative way. "That's why it was in your briefcase, Sir. They just love to creep into warm, dark places – like pockets, Sir. Or underneath your jumper."

"*Aaargh!*"

Eric stared in amazement as Mr Perry galloped towards the staffroom.

"What's wrong with him? I was only being helpful."

Adam picked up his snake.

Eric got the list from behind his ear.

He unfolded it again. He frowned. "Pet swapping day is really complicated," he told his white rat, who was perched on his shoulder, like a parrot.

Eric smoothed the list out on his knee. He took a pencil from behind his other ear. The pencil broke. He borrowed one from Adam. He altered the list in big, shaky letters.

~~One~~

~~Two~~ grass snakes

Two

It's really tiring being efficient, thought Eric, tucking the list back safely behind his ear. He liked being in charge. But he was quite glad Corinne was only away for one lesson.

"By the way," he asked Adam, as they filed back into the classroom, "what is the next lesson? I always forget."

"Next lesson's swimming," said Adam.

"Oh, dear," said Eric. His face scrunched into a frown. Pet swapping day was just about to get even more complicated.

When Class Six walked to the swimming-pool, passers-by kept out of their way. You could see why. One boy was wrestling with a snake. It kept

coiling up his arm. Another had strange, moveable lumps under his clothes. A worried girl was holding a paper bag at arm's length.

She said to her friend, "I don't think I should have swapped these. He told me they could turn nasty."

"Why do we have to go to this horrible swimming-pool?" said Adam to Eric. "Nobody goes to this one. Why can't we go to the Leisure Centre? It's only just down the road. And it's got a wave machine. And flumes and everything! Nelson Street Baths hasn't even got a diving board! It's the pits!"

It was true. The Leisure Centre was bright and clean and cheery. But Nelson Street Baths was an ancient building that looked like a prison.

The changing-rooms were dark and damp and smelly. They were painted a sickly green. The chlorine made your eyes water – and that was even before you climbed into the pool.

"Don't ask me," said Eric. "If we went to the Leisure Centre I bet I wouldn't be scared of the water. Not like I am at Nelson Street."

Chapter 4

Ten minutes later, Eric was shivering by the side of the pool. He wore baggy swimming trunks. He was hugging his bony body tight. Eric hated swimming lessons at Nelson Street Baths.

But at least, he thought, Corinne would be proud of him. Pet swapping day was going like a dream. The animals were all safely shut away in lockers in the changing-room. Eric had seen to it himself – personally.

There's no way, he thought proudly, that they're going to escape from THERE!

Then, he had no time to think about anything else. For Mrs Foster, their swimming teacher, came bounding out from the changing-rooms. She was a muscular person in a black swimsuit covered in badges.

"Class dive in!" she bellowed, blowing her whistle.

Thirty bodies hit the water with a thunderous crash. All except Eric, who was still trembling at the top of the steps.

"I'm all splashed now!" complained Eric, shaking water out of his hair like a wet dog.

"Swim across!" Mrs Foster ordered Class Six. Her booming voice echoed around the pool. "*Across, across, across!*"

Sixty arms went like windmills. After what seemed like hours of splashing Class Six made it across. They clung on to the side, exhausted.

"Come on, Eric!" urged Mrs Foster. She slapped him encouragingly on the back. Eric crumpled to the floor, coughing.

"You can do it! Just watch me!" And Mrs Foster dived like an arrow into the pool. She began to swim across, with a powerful breast-stroke.

"Whoops!" said Eric.

A long, glistening streak was gliding through the water. It was heading straight for Mrs Foster.

"Whoops!" said Eric again. "How did that escape? I checked those lockers myself!"

There was a blood-curdling shriek. Mrs Foster had seen the grass snake. She splashed at it, wildly. The pool filled with waves.

"*AAARGH!*" cried Mrs Foster. She had seen something else. Bobbing towards her on the crest of a wave were eight froggy eyes.

"My rat's escaped as well!" cried Eric, pointing.

There had been a mass break-out of pets!

"Not my fault!" said Eric to no one in particular. "I couldn't help it!"

Eric's white rat swam past Mrs Foster doing a very efficient doggy paddle. He flashed her a quick smile with his wicked little teeth and swam on.

"Help!" cried Mrs Foster. "Help!"

"It's only a grass snake!" Eric called out helpfully. "It's not an adder. It won't hurt you!"

Mrs Foster splashed frantically towards the side and safety. Four frogs swam with her like a synchronized swimming team. They were grinning all over their silly froggy faces.

Chapter 5

At lunchtime Corinne came back from the dentist's.

"What's been going on?" she asked Eric sternly. "I left you in charge of pet swapping day. And you've made a complete mess of it. *And* the swimming-pool had to be evacuated. *And* Mrs Foster's gone home with a headache. *And* Mr Perry says he never wants to teach children ever again! *And*, by the way, where's my list?"

Eric felt behind his ear. He pulled out a grey, soggy ball of paper. "Whoops," he said. "It's got a bit wet. Must've been when I got splashed, at the swimming-pool."

"I don't suppose it matters," said Corinne. "There are no pets left anyway! They've all escaped!"

"I caught my rat," said Eric. A whiskery face poked out of his collar and winked at Corinne with clever pink eyes.

"And I've still got my dung-beetles," said the tiny boy, hopefully, holding up his matchbox.

But Corinne ignored him. She tapped her foot.

"I'm waiting," she said to Eric in a dangerous voice. "Waiting for an explanation. And *don't* say it's not your fault."

"Errrr," said Eric. "Errrr." Then he ran away and hid in the boys' toilets.

The next day Eric crept into school at the last minute. He was trying to avoid Corinne. He still couldn't explain how a simple thing like pet swapping day had turned into such a major muddle.

He climbed into the school yard over a fence.

"Whoops!" said Eric.

For there was Corinne, waiting for him.

But she didn't look dangerous. She didn't even look stern. Instead she said, smiling: "Well done, Eric!"

"Whaaaaaaa?" said Eric, his mouth hanging open. "What?"

"You have done a brilliant thing!" said Corinne.

Eric looked around. But she wasn't talking to anyone else. She was talking to him!

"Have I?" asked Eric, confused.

"Of course!" said Corinne. "Just look at this newspaper. Read this bit!"

Eric followed Corinne's finger. He read the words out loud. "NELSON STREET BATHS INVADED BY VERMIN," the newspaper said. "'The old buildings are to blame,' said Councillor Duckett. 'They must be shut down immediately!'"

Still Eric's face wore a puzzled frown.

"Don't you see?" said Corinne. "It means we can't go swimming there any more. The headmaster said so. We're going to the Leisure Centre, starting next week!"

"Yes," said Adam, "with wave machines and flumes and things! And machines where you can buy sweets!"

"Brilliant!" said someone else, slapping Eric on the back.

Everyone crowded round. Eric was the class hero. "It was nothing," he said modestly. But, secretly, his chest swelled with pride. It was the best day of his life, so far.

"You can be in charge of next pet swapping day, if you like," said Corinne generously.

"Er, no thanks," said Eric. "I think I'll leave it to you."

A girl joined the crowd. She was holding a paper bag at arm's length. It rustled and jumped in a very sinister manner.

"Do you want to swap these for those dung-beetles?" she said to the boy with the matchbox.

"See!" said the dung-beetle boy to Corinne. "I told you someone would want my beetles. I told you they were lovely."

Rather reluctantly, he handed over the matchbox. "Mind you look after them," he said. "Mind you give them a fresh cow-pat every week."

The girl handed over the paper bag. She seemed very pleased indeed to get rid of it. She began rushing away, before the boy could change his mind.

"Wait a minute!" the new owner of the paper bag called after her. "What kind of pets are they, exactly? I mean, exactly what's inside this paper bag?"

"I don't know," the girl called back.
"I was too scared to open it. He told
me they could turn nasty." And she
vanished into the playground crowd.

BRINGGG! BRINGGG!

School had started. Eric, beaming all over his face, was carried into school by Class Six.

"Three cheers for Eric!" called Corinne.

"Hurray! Hurray! Hurray!"

Eric's white rat poked his face out of Eric's pocket. He grinned at the cheering crowd.

"And I've decided," announced Eric, "that I'm not going to swap my white rat. I like him too much. He's almost like part of me! So I'm going to keep him – always."

"*Squeak, squeak,*" went Eric's white rat as he dived down Eric's jumper.

The tiny boy with the paper bag walked slowly into school. He was holding the bag at arm's length. The bag twitched and rustled in an alarming way. The boy screwed the top of the bag more tightly shut. He had a very worried look on his face.

"I think," he said, "that I want my dung-beetles back."

The End

Author's note: Pet Swapping Day is only a story. Please do not take your own pets to school to swap!